DUDLEY SCHOOLS LIBRARY
AND INFORMATION SERVICE

KU-345-346

Schools Library and Information Services

S00000676204

THIS ORCHARD
BOOK BELONGS TO

_____

DUDLEY SCHOOLS LIBRARY
AND INFORMATION SERVICE

_____

_____

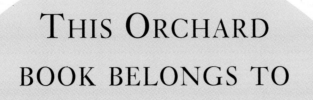

To my Lara – H.O.

For Hugo – V.C.

ORCHARD BOOKS

338 Euston Road, London NW1 3BH

Orchard Books Australia

Hachette Children's Books

17/207 Kent Street, Sydney NSW 2000

1 84362 872 4

First published in Great Britain in 2006

Text © Hiawyn Oram 2006

Illustrations © Vanessa Cabban 2006

The right of Hiawyn Oram to be identified as the author and Vanessa Cabban to be identified
as the illustrator of this work has been asserted by them in accordance
with the Copyright, Designs and Patents Act 1988.

A CIP catalogue record for this book is available from the British Library.

2 4 6 8 10 9 7 5 3 1

Printed in China

DUDLEY PUBLIC LIBRARIES

L

676204 | BCH

JY ORA

WHEN WISHING COMES TRUE

HIAWYN ORAM ❀ VANESSA CABBAN

ORCHARD BOOKS

Once there were
two good friends, Tom and Tansy.

One day, lying by the river, Tansy said,

"Tom, does wishing come true?"

"Don't know," said Tom.

"Let's try it and see."

So up they sat, closed
their eyes and wished.

Tansy wished for a party dress,
party shoes and a dance to dance at.

Tom wished to sail away

in a boat and see the world.

Though they wished hard and though they
wished long, when they opened their eyes,
there was no dress, no shoes, no dance,
no boat and no chance to see the world.

"Well, there you are," said Tansy.

"Wishing doesn't come true."

"But wait!" cried Tom. "What's that?"

It was Mr Grimpalong, limping along,
pushing his cart full of any old stuff
and singing,

"Any old stuff, give or take,

Take or give, any old stuff."

"Wow," said Tom. "What luck! Any
old stuff might be all we need!"

"Hello!" called Mr Grimpalong. "I was just wishing this cart was lighter and now I've met you it will be."

And from the cart he took this and that, a bit of whatsit, a lot of whatever and a large pair of scissors.

"And what do you know!" he smiled.

"It's all for you."

"But isn't it a lot of rubbish?" said Tansy.

"No, no!" said Mr G. "With some of this and a bit of that, Tom could make a raft, sail down the river and see the world!"

"That's funny," said Tom, "that's just what I wished!"

"Good!" said Mr Grimpalong. "And, Tansy, with a bit of this, some of that, a snip snip here and a whirr whirr there, you could make a dress and shoes to dance in!"

"That's funny," said Tansy,
"that's just what I wished!"

"Well, there you are," said Mr G.

"And now, as my cart's empty and I've nothing more to push, I'll give you a hand – then I'll take a rest as I've always wished to do!"

So Tom, Tansy and Mr Grimpalong got to work.

Saw, saw, saw. Hammer, hammer, hammer.

Rub-a-dub-rub. Snip, snap, snip.

Whirr, whirr, whirr.

Plink, hum, saw – saw a bit more.

Plank-plunk-bang.

And before long . . .

Tom had a raft with
a sail and two paddles.

Tansy had a dress and
some dancing shoes.

And Mr Grimpalong had time to lie in
the shade and watch the clouds go by.
"Good cloud-watching, Mr G!"
called Tom. "All aboard, Tansy!"

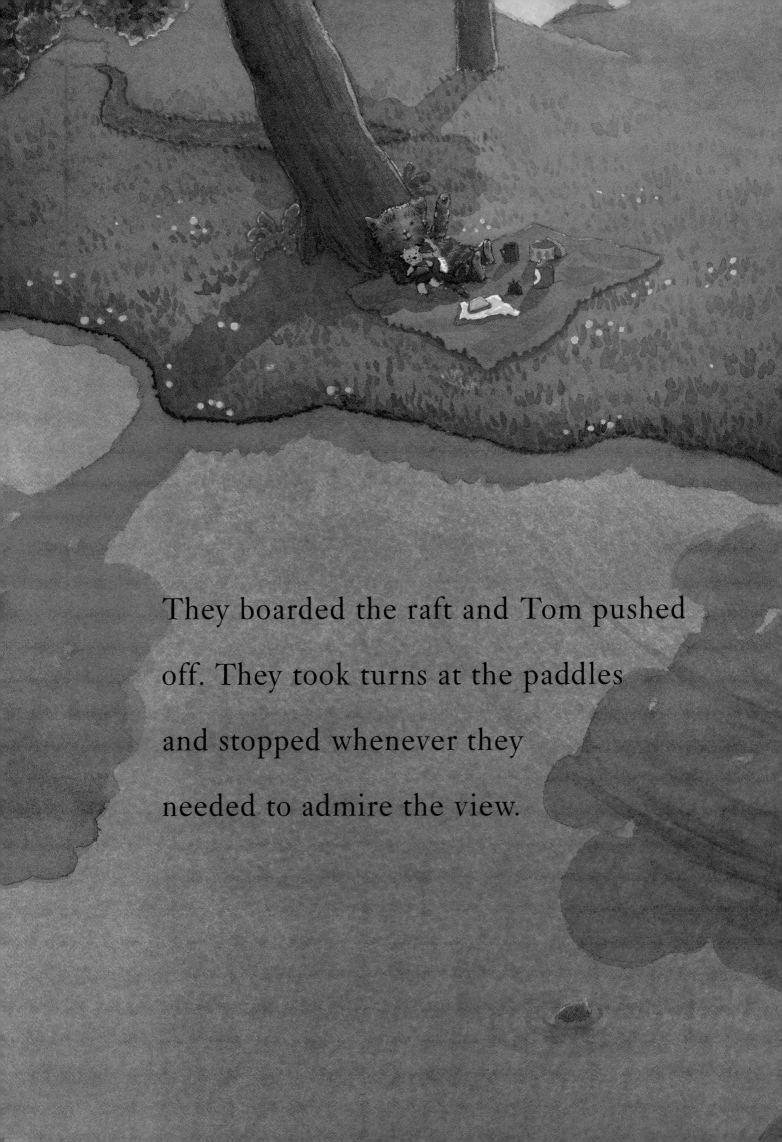

They boarded the raft and Tom pushed
off. They took turns at the paddles
and stopped whenever they
needed to admire the view.

"Ho ho!" cried Tom. "Got the boat,
got the paddles, and seeing the world,
just as I wished . . .

. . . and what a wonderful world it

turns out to be."

"And I'm hearing music!" said Tansy.

And round the bend they found a river
boat. On the boat was a band of fiddlers,
fiddling tunes, merry as could be.

"Hello," called the first fiddler. "Would
you join our dance? Please, feel free!"

"Tee hee!" laughed Tansy. "Got the dress, got the shoes, found a dance to dance at, just as I wished."

And, much much later, when Tom had looked at the world as long as he wished, and Tansy's dancing shoes had nearly worn out, Tom said, "Time to get back and tell Mr G all about it."

So they turned the raft round

and paddled home.

As they paddled, they were quiet
as quiet, each thinking the same
quiet thought about wishing.

And that quiet thought was this –

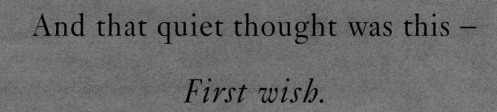

First wish.

Then do.

That's when wishing comes true.